Rhyme Time
VALENTINE

Nancy Poydar

Holiday House / New York

Library of Congress Cataloging-in-Publication Data
Poydar, Nancy.
Rhyme time valentine / by Nancy Poydar.—1st ed.
p. cm.
Summary: Ruby's homemade valentines blow away while she is walking to school,
but she figures out a way to give everyone a valentine anyway.
ISBN 0-8234-1684-4 (hardcover)
[1. Valentines—Fiction. 2. Valentine's Day—Fiction.
3. Rhyme—Fiction. 4. Schools—Fiction.]
I. Title.
PZ7.P8846 Rh 2002
[E]—dc21   2001024113

Roses are red.
Violets are blue.
Dear Jolene,
this book is for you.
Love, Nancy

Ruby loved Valentine's Day.
"My favorite color is red.
I know how to cut a valentine out of folded paper.
I can read the words on candy hearts."
Ruby couldn't stop talking about Valentine's Day.

Room Nine was getting ready.
They were decorating boxes to collect their valentines.
They were making rhymes.
Even Mr. Lister was decorating a box.

Roses are red.
Violets are blue.
I have a valentine
for each
of you.

Anthony was signing his valentines.
"Anthony, Anthony, Anthony..."
"My valentines are cartoons," boasted Lucy.

"I *made* my cards two days ago," Ruby said.
"With rhymes! *And* I'm going to wear all red
tomorrow: red top, red bottom, red tights.
I even have a red name!"

When Valentine's Day came, it was gray.
"A good day to stay in bed," said Ruby's dad.
Ruby thought hard.
"Roses are red.
Violets are blue.
Don't stay in bed.
There's too much to do!" she chimed.

Roses are red.
Violets are blue.
My best valentine
is for you.
Love, Ruby

There was a box for Ruby.
"Candy hearts! **BE MINE**," she read. "Mmmmm."
Then she gave her parents a paper heart.
"Sweet!" said Ruby's mom.

Ruby's coat wasn't red, so she opened it.
Her red skirt swirled in the wind.
Her red boots shone in the wet.

The bag with her homemade valentines
slapped against her leg. The wind got stronger.
The sky spit snow.
"Blow, snow!" commanded Ruby.

Whip, dip, went the wind.

Yay, yay,
for Valentine's Day.
Love, Ruby

Wap, SNAP, went the bag.
Flutter, flutter,
went the paper valentines.

"Come back!" cried Ruby.

Be mine,
Valentine.
Love, Ruby

"Hurry up!" called Anthony.
"You're late."

Ruby was too mad to run.

"Too bad," said Lucy.
"Bad, sad," rhymed Ruby.
Woosh, wish, went the wind.
"I wish that someone
could get my valentines,"
sputtered Ruby.

"Rhyme time!" said Mr. Lister. He wrote *red*.
"Dead!" shouted Anthony.

"Good," said Mr. Lister. "Ruby, you always have a rhyme."
"Bed," muttered Ruby. "I should have stayed in bed."
Nine, wrote Mr. Lister.
"Mine," said Emily.
"Valentine," mumbled Ruby.

Room Nine had indoor recess.

"I'll make more valentines," Ruby decided.
She fiddled with the colored paper. No more red!
She cut some hearts out of orange.
Clip, snip, went the scissors.
"Pumpkins?" guessed Anthony.

Clip, snip. She tried the green.
"Leaves?" asked Emily.

Clip, snip. She tried the purple.
"Plums!" said Lucy. "Plums aren't for Valentine's Day."

"Dumb, plum!" grumbled Ruby. Recess was over.
Ruby stuffed her hands into her pockets.

The candy hearts!

"**SWEET TALK**," read Ruby.
"**SO GOOD**," read Ruby.
"Time to deliver our valentines,"
announced Mr. Lister.

Anthony liked candy.
"**SMILE**," read Ruby.
"Yummm," said Anthony.

Lucy skipped by.
"**DEAR HEART**," read Ruby.
"Thanks," said Lucy.

Emily looked hungry.
"**ONLY YOU,**" read Ruby.
"Mmmmm," said Emily.

"**BABY, BABY**," read Mr. Lister.
"**SWEET TREAT**," read Jack.
"**HIGH FIVE**," read Ruby.

"Ruby, look outside!" called Anthony.

Someone in Room Nine
Wants to be your

I hate coffee.
I hate tea.
I like you.
Do you like

Loop, swoop,
came Ruby's paper hearts,
swirling, twirling through the air.

Dear teach
You're a pea

Valentine's Day is the best.
I like it better than the

Roses are red.
Violets are blue.
My silliest heart
goes to

"COOL," read Anthony.
"AWESOME," read Ruby.

Hush, went the wind.

✂ Ruby's Valentine

You will need colored paper, a pencil, and scissors.

1. Take a rectangular or square piece of paper.

2. Fold it in half.

3. Draw a petal-shaped half heart with the straight edge along the fold.

4. Cut it out and open up your heart!

5. Decorate your heart.

AWESOME!